O9-AHW-453

Gulliver's Travels

*Retold from the Jonathan Swift
original by Martin Woodside*

Illustrated by Jamel Akib

STERLING

New York / London
www.sterlingpublishing.com/kids

STERLING and the distinctive Sterling logo are registered trademarks of
Sterling Publishing Co., Inc.

Library of Congress Cataloging-in-Publication Data

Woodside, Martin.
  Gulliver's travels / retold from the Jonathan Swift original ; abridged by
Martin Woodside ; illustrated by Jamel Akib.
    p. cm.—Classic starts)
Summary : An abridged version of the voyages of an eighteenth-century
Englishman that carry him to such strange places as Lilliput, where people
are six inches tall, and Brobdingnag, a land peopled by giants.
  ISBN 1-4027-2662-7
1. Voyages and travels—Fiction. 2. Fantasy.] I. Akib, Jamel, ill. II. Swift,
Jonathan, 1667–1745. Gulliver's travels. III. Title. IV. Series.

PZ7.W867Gul 2006
[Fic]—dc22

                                                              2005015766

                        4 6 8 10 9 7 5

                 Published by Sterling Publishing Co., Inc.
                387 Park Avenue South, New York, NY 10016
                   Copyright © 2006 by Martin Woodside
                 Illustrations copyright © 2006 by Jamel Akib
                  Distributed in Canada by Sterling Publishing
               ᶜ/ₒ Canadian Manda Group, 165 Dufferin Street
                     Toronto, Ontario, Canada M6K 3H6
         Distributed in Great Britain and Europe by Chris Lloyd at Orca Book
           Services, Stanley House, Fleets Lane, Poole BH15 3AJ, England
           Distributed in Australia by Capricorn Link (Australia) Pty. Ltd.
                    P.O. Box 704, Windsor, NSW 2756, Australia

              Classic Starts is a trademark of Sterling Publishing Co., Inc.

                              Printed in China
                             All rights reserved
                           Designed by Renato Stanisic

                    Sterling ISBN 978-1-4027-2662-0

      For information about custom editions, special sales, premium and
         corporate purchases, please contact Sterling Special Sales
      Department at 800-805-5489 or specialsales@sterlingpublishing.com.

CONTENTS

CHAPTER 1

*The author gives some account of himself and
his desire to travel. He is shipwrecked and arrives on
shore in the country of Lilliput.*

೧

I was raised on a small country estate in England.
After my studies, I worked under a surgeon in
London and set to learning what I could of navigation and mathematics.

It would not do to trouble the reader with all
the details of my youth. It is enough to know that
my plan was to travel, and at the age of twenty-
two, I left for sea. After three and a half years, I
returned to London and married Mrs. Mary
Burton. I planned to settle down then, but my
greatest voyages, it seemed, still lay ahead of me.

I accepted an offer to serve upon the *Antelope,* which was making a voyage to the South Seas. We were in passage to the East Indies when a violent storm struck the ship. Twelve of our crew died and the rest were in very weak condition when the wind drove us upon a large rock, splitting the ship.

I swam, as fate intended, and by that evening I reached shore. I lay down on the grass, which was very short and soft, and there I slept more soundly than I ever had in my life.

It was just daylight when I awoke. I tried to stand but found that I was unable to move. I was lying on my back with my arms and legs strongly tied to the ground. I felt several slender ropes binding me from my armpits to my thighs. The sun grew hot and the light began to blind me. I could make out a confused noise about me, but could see nothing but the sky.

In a little while, I felt something moving on

my left leg. It walked gently forward over my breast and almost up to my chin. Bending my head as much as I could, I saw that it was a human creature, not six inches high, with a bow and arrow in his hand and a quiver on his back. I felt several more of these creatures following the path of the first. I was shocked and roared so loud that the creatures all ran back in fright. Some of them, I was told later, were hurt by their falls.

However, they soon returned. One of them, who ventured so far as to get in full sight of my face, cried out in a shrill but distinct voice: *Hekinah Degul!*

The others repeated those words several times, but I knew not what they meant. I managed to break the strings that fastened my left arm to the ground and loosen the strings that tied down my hair. I could now turn my head about two inches. There was a great shout in a very shrill accent and I heard one of them cry aloud: *Tolgo Phonac!*

An instant later, I felt a hundred arrows shot into my left hand. The arrows pricked me like needles. The men shot another round of arrows into the air, many of which fell on my body (though I felt them not) and some on my face, which I covered with my free hand.

I decided it was best to lie still. My plan was to stay that way until night when, my left hand already being loose, I could easily free myself. As for the inhabitants, I had reason to believe I might be a match for the greatest armies they could bring against me, if they were all of the same size as those I had already seen.

But fortune had other plans for me. The arrows stopped coming. I listened and, by the increasing noise, knew that their numbers were greater. Just above my right ear, I heard a great knocking that lasted about an hour. Turning my head that way, I saw a stage being built about a foot and a half from the ground. It was capable of holding four of the inhabitants, with two or three ladders to mount it.

The strings that fastened the left side of my head were cut, allowing me to turn my head and see the stage fully. From this stage, one of the creatures made a long speech that I couldn't understand. The speaker was only slightly taller than my middle finger

I answered him in a few words. Being almost starved, I couldn't help putting my finger to my mouth to show that I wanted food. The speaker descended from the stage and commanded that several ladders be applied to my sides. From there, a hundred or so of the inhabitants climbed up and walked toward my mouth carrying baskets of meat and bread. I ate them, by two or three baskets at a mouthful. They supplied me as fast as they could, showing great wonder at my appetite. Afterward, they filled one of their largest canteens with water—holding no more than half a pint—and rolled it toward my hand. I drained it quickly and they filled the canteen twice more for me to drink.

When I was finished, they shouted for joy and danced upon my chest, yelling repeatedly: *Hekinah Degul!*

After eating and drinking my fill, I became drowsy. The cords were loosened so that I could turn on my side and I quickly fell asleep. I slept for about eight hours, greatly helped by a sleeping potion, which I later found out had been mixed into my water.

While I slept, a great machine fixed on wheels was built to move me to the capital city. Nine hundred of the city's strongest men were needed to raise me and I was tied into place on the engine. I slept through all of this and was about four hours into our journey when I awoke.

The carriage finally stopped at the sight of an abandoned temple, which was the largest building in the whole kingdom. The great gate in the front was about four feet high and almost two feet wide. I could easily crawl inside. On each side of the gate was a small window, not six inches from the ground. Through that eleven chains were fed and chained to my left leg.

The chains that held my left leg were about two yards long and gave me only the freedom of walking backward and forward in a semicircle. Being fixed within four inches of the gate, the chains allowed me to crawl in and lie at my full length in the temple. My strings had been cut loose and I got up, feeling as sad as I ever had in my life.

CHAPTER 2

*The emperor of Lilliput comes to see
the author and educated men are chosen to teach
the author their language. The author asks for his
freedom and it is granted.*

⌒

When I found myself on my feet, I looked about me and must confess that I never saw a more entertaining sight. The country around me looked like a large garden. The fenced in fields, which were generally 40 feet square, resembled many beds of flowers. These fields were mixed with woods of half an acre. The tallest trees, as I could judge, appeared to be seven feet high. I viewed the town to my left, which looked like the painted scene of a city in a theater.

The emperor appeared before me on horseback

with his guards close by. The horses were quite frightened at the sight of me, but the emperor managed to calm them. The emperor was taller than his men by almost the width of a nail. His features were strong and masculine. He was then twenty-eight years old and had reigned for seven years in great happiness. His dress was very simple, but he had on his head a light helmet of gold and jewels. He had his sword drawn, prepared to defend himself should I break loose.

His Majesty spoke to me and I answered, though neither of us could understand a word. He had several advisors and lawyers, or so I assumed by their behavior, who were commanded to talk to me. I tried to speak with them in as many languages as I knew the least bit of—including Dutch, Latin, French, Spanish, and Italian—but all to no effect. After two hours, the court departed and I was left with a strong guard, in part to keep curious crowds away.

Toward night, I crawled into my house with little difficulty and laid on the ground. I slept this way for a week, during which time the emperor had a bed made for me. The finished product was made of a hundred and fifty of their beds sewn together in length and width.

Every morning forty sheep and other foods were delivered to me, along with an equal amount of bread and water. Six hundred people were put to work as my servants and it was ordered that three hundred tailors should make me a suit of clothes in the fashion of their country. Finally, six of His Majesty's greatest teachers were hired to help me learn their language

Within my first three weeks there, I made great progress in learning their language. The emperor honored me often with his visits and we began to speak together in some sort. The first thing I did was ask for my freedom, a desire I repeated to him every day on my knees. He answered that this would take time, but he promised to treat me kindly and advised me to be patient.

His Majesty also voiced his concerns that I carried several weapons with me. He asked me to give up my sword, which now had some rust on it from the salt water, and my pocket pistols. At his desire, I showed the emperor how the pistols worked and warned him not to be afraid when I fired the pistol into the air. Still, hundreds fell down as if struck dead. Even the emperor, though he stood his ground, looked quite pale.

I did everything I could to gain their trust and the natives came to be less and less afraid of me. I would sometimes lie down and let five or six of them dance on my hand. The boys and girls would play hide and seek in my hair. The horses of the royal stables were no longer scared of me but would come right up to my feet.

Meanwhile, I had sent so many requests for

my freedom that His Majesty discussed the matter at length, first in his cabinet and then in the council. It was opposed by none, except a man named Skyresh Bolgolam, who was pleased to be my enemy for no reason.

Skyresh was at length persuaded to agree but demanded that conditions should be set upon my freedom. I was made to swear to these in the method set out by their laws. I had to hold my right foot in my left hand, place the middle finger of my right hand on the crown of my head, and place my thumb on the tip of my ear. I have made a translation of the whole of these articles, as near as I was able, which I here offer to the public:

"Golbasto Momaren Evlame Gurdilo Shefin Mully Ully Gue, most mighty emperor of Lilliput, delight and terror of the universe, whose dimensions extend five blustrugs (about twelve miles of circumference) to the ends of the globe; ruler of all rulers; taller than the sons of men;

whose feet press down to the center of the Earth and whose head strikes against the sun; at whose nod the princes of the earth shake their knees; pleasant as the spring, comfortable as the summer, fruitful as autumn, dreadful as winter. His Majesty proposes to the man-mountain, lately arrived in our country, the following articles, which by sincere promise he shall be made to perform.

First, the man-mountain shall not leave our country without our permission under our Great Seal.

Second, he shall not come into our city without our specific order. At such time as he enters the city, the inhabitants shall have two hours warning to keep within their doors.

Third, the said man-mountain shall limit his walks to our high roads and not offer to walk or lie down in a meadow or field of corn.

Fourth, as he walks the said roads, he shall take the utmost care not to step on the bodies of any of our loving subjects, their horses, or carriages, nor take any of our subjects into his hands without their own consent.

Fifth, if a delivery is required, the man-mountain shall carry in his pocket the messenger and horse on a six-day journey, once a month, and return the said messenger back (if so required) safely to our Imperial Presence.

Sixth, he shall be our friend against our enemies in the island of Blefuscu and do his best to destroy their fleet that is now preparing to invade us.

Seventh, that the said man-mountain shall, at his times of rest, assist our workmen in helping to raise certain great stones toward covering the wall of the principal park, and other of our royal buildings.

Eighth, that the said man-mountain shall, in two months' time, measure the exact boundary of our country.

Lastly, that upon his sincere promise to observe all the above articles, the said man-mountain shall have a daily allowance of meat and drink equal to the support needed for 1,728 of our subjects, with free access to our royal person, and other marks of our favor. Given at our palace at Belfaborac the twelfth day of the ninety-first year of our reign."

I swore to these articles with great cheerfulness, although some of the conditions were not as honorable as I could have wished. Afterward, my chains were unlocked and I was free. I made my acknowledgments by kneeling at His Majesty's feet. He commanded me to rise. He said that I should prove a useful servant and was well deserving of his favor.

CHAPTER 3

Mildendo, the capital city of Lilliput,
is described. The author prevents an invasion and
great honor is given to him.

⌐∽

The first request I made after getting my freedom was that I might be able to see Mildendo, the
capital city. The emperor granted this easily, with
the promise that I do no harm to the inhabitants
or their houses.

The wall that ran around the city was two and
a half feet tall and at least eleven inches wide, bor-
dered by strong towers some ten feet apart. I
stepped over the western gate and passed very
gently, moving sideways through the two main

streets, walking carefully to avoid anyone who remained on the streets.

The emperor's palace was in the center of the city, where the two great streets met. It was surrounded by a wall that was two feet tall and twenty feet away from the buildings. The outward court was forty feet around and included two other courts; in the inmost courts were the royal apartments, which I was very eager to see but found it very hard to get to.

About a week after I had been given my freedom, the emperor's secretary came to my house and asked to speak to me privately. I offered to lie down so that he might more easily reach my ear, but he chose rather to let me hold him in my hand during our conversation.

He began by congratulating me on getting my freedom, but added that it might not have been granted so easily if not for certain events at court.

For the last two months, he said, the island of Blefuscu had been threatening to invade them. I had told them about many nations populated by creatures of the same size as myself, but the only nations known to them were Blefuscu and Lilliput. These two countries had been at war for nearly seven years. The war had begun over the issue of eggs.

It had been taken for granted for some time that the proper way to eat an egg involved breaking it open at the larger end. The present emperor's grandfather had cut his finger eating an egg in this way and, afterward, it was commanded that all subjects break their eggs open at the smaller end. The people disliked this law so much that six rebellions were formed. One emperor lost his life and another lost his crown. It was reckoned that eleven thousand people suffered death rather than submit to breaking their eggs at the smaller end. The royal family of Blefuscu did their best to stir up these rebels and many people fled to that kingdom

Those people had grown so powerful in the court of Blefuscu that a bloody war began over the egg issue. Thousands of lives had already been lost and, now, Blefuscu had prepared a large fleet and was getting ready to make its descent upon Lilliput. For that reason, His Imperial Majesty was asking for my help.

The enemy fleet consisted of about fifty men-of-war and a great number of transport ships. I put out an order for bars of iron and a large amount of the strongest cable available. The cable was about as thick as thread and the iron bars were the size of knitting needles. I doubled the thread and twisted three of the bars together, bending the ends into a hook. Having prepared fifty hooks, I headed for the coast.

Taking off my coat, shoes, and stockings, I

walked into the sea. I swam until my feet touched the ground again and arrived at the fleet in less than half an hour. The enemy was so frightened to see me that they leaped out of their ships and swam to shore. I then took my hooks and fastened one to each of the ships. While I was doing this, the enemy shot several thousand arrows at me, which greatly disturbed my work. Luckily, I had taken the trouble of putting on my glasses, as my greatest fear was that one of the arrows would strike me in the eye.

With all the knots fastened, I began to pull. I drew the enemy's men-of-war behind me with great ease. When the Blefuscudians saw me pulling their whole fleet away, they let out a scream of grief and despair that it is almost impossible to describe or understand.

I arrived safe at the royal port of Lilliput an hour later. The emperor and his whole court stood on the shore, expecting my arrival. When I

got within hearing range, I held up the cable and shouted in a loud voice:

"Long live the most powerful Emperor of Lilliput!"

The emperor was overjoyed. He planned to use me to reduce all of Blefuscu into a mere province, to destroy the exiles, to make the people break the smaller part of the egg, and to become the ruler of the whole world. When I heard this, I said that I would never be the instrument of bringing a free and brave people into slavery. When the matter was debated in council, the wisest part of the ministry was in agreement with me.

The emperor would never forgive me, though. From this time on, there was a plot between His Majesty and a group of ministers who wished me ill. In less than two months, this plot grew strong enough to nearly bring about my total ruin. Such is the price of refusing to grant the wishes of a prince.

Three weeks after my daring act, a group of

ambassadors arrived from Blefuscu with humble offerings of peace. Conditions were soon agreed upon that proved very good for our emperor. When their treaty was finished, the ambassadors paid me a visit. They had privately been told of the service I had done them and wished to thank me. They complimented me on my great bravery and kindness, and invited me to visit their kingdom.

I asked the emperor's permission to visit Blefuscu, which he was pleased to grant. His manner was very cold, but I could not then guess the reason why.

CHAPTER 4

The author, being told of a plan to accuse him of high treason, makes his escape to Blefuscu.

I should provide the reader with some description of this curious empire. The common height of the natives is somewhat less than six inches. The tallest horses and oxen are between four and five inches, and the tallest sheep are about an inch and a half tall. The Lilliputians bury their dead with their heads directly downward because they hold the opinion that in eleven thousand years they will all rise again. At this point, the earth, which they believe to be flat, will turn upside down. Buried this way, they believe that they will be found standing on their feet again.

I learned of this custom in the nine months and thirteen days that I stayed in that country. I might have stayed longer, if not for the plot that was forming against me.

Just as I was preparing to visit the emperor of Blefuscu, a respectable person at court secretly came to my house and asked to speak with me.

After the common greetings, he told me that Skyresh Bolgolam had gathered supporters and that they had prepared articles of accusation against me for treason and other crimes. Out of gratitude for my help with Blefuscu, this good man had brought me information about these dealings and a copy of the articles themselves. I have made a translation of these, which I now offer to the public.

Articles of accusation Against Quinbus Flestrin,
(the man-mountain)

ARTICLE 1

That the said Quinbus Flestrin brought
the imperial fleet of Blefuscu into the
royal port. He was afterward commanded
by His Imperial Majesty to take all the
other ships of the empire of Blefuscu and
reduce that empire to a province, and to
destroy and put to death all of the exiles.
The Flestrin, like a false traitor, asked to be
excused from said service claiming unwillingness to destroy the freedoms and lives
of an innocent people.

ARTICLE 2

That when certain ambassadors arrived
from the court of Blefuscu to arrange the
peace, the Flestrin did help the ambassadors

although he knew them to be servants of a prince who was recently an open enemy to His Majesty.

ARTICLE 3

That the said Quinbus Flestrin is now preparing to make a voyage to the court of Blefuscu, for which he has received only verbal permission from His Majesty. Also, that he falsely and disloyally intends to help the emperor of Blefuscu, who was recently an open enemy of His Imperial Majesty.

There were several other articles, but these were the most important. Skyresh and his supporters insisted that I should be put to death by setting my house on fire at night. Then the general was supposed to have twenty thousand men shoot me with poisoned arrows in the face and hands.

His Majesty's secretary urged mercy, the best

characteristic in a prince. He asked His Majesty to be happy with merely putting out both of my eyes and sparing my life. This way, he said, I would still be able to use my bodily strength to serve His Majesty.

He suggested that, if blinding proved to weak a punishment, I could be starved to death by slowly lessening my supply of food. Upon my death, five or six thousand of His Majesty's subjects might cut my flesh from my bones and bury it in distant parts to avoid infections, leaving the skeleton as a reminder of my actions. This plan was agreed to by all. It was decided that the sentence of blinding would be made public while the plan to starve me would be kept secret.

This conclusion was thought to be an example of His Majesty's s great compassion. I must confess that I could not see the mercy in this sentence, but rather found it to be quite harsh. I thought of standing trial to defend myself, but having seen many trials, figured this was a risky option. I could easily destroy the entire empire, but I soon rejected this idea with horror. Finally I decided on my course of action.

Before the three days had passed, I sent a letter to my friend the secretary, informing him of my plan to set out that morning for Blefuscu. Without waiting for a reply, I went to the coast where our fleet lay. Putting all of my belongings in a large man-of-war, I dragged it behind me and half waded, half swam to Blefuscu.

The people had long expected me there. Within an hour of my arrival, His Majesty, joined by the royal family and the great officers of court, came out to greet me. I told His Majesty that I had arrived as promised, not mentioning a word of my situation. I was received well by the court but, lacking a house and bed, was forced to sleep on the ground with only a blanket.

CHAPTER 5

The author, by a lucky accident, finds means to leave
Blefuscu and returns to his natural country.

✧

Three days after my arrival, I was walking out to the northeast end of the island and saw some way off what looked like a rowboat overturned in the sea. I waded two or three hundred yards out and found the object to be a real boat, which I supposed had been driven from some ship in a storm.

I returned immediately to His Majesty and asked him to lend me twenty of the tallest ships he had left and three thousand of his seamen under the command of his vice admiral. The ships sailed around while I went back to the coast where I first discovered the boat.

The tide had driven the boat even closer. When the ships came up, I stripped myself and waded in until I came within a hundred yards of the rowboat, after which I was forced to swim to it. The seamen had been given a lot of cords. They tossed me the ends of the cords, which I fastened to a hole in the front part of the boat. I swam behind the boat, pushing, while the ships towed. Finally we got within forty yards of the shore. We waited there until the tide had gone out and the boat had been left on the sand. Turning the boat over, I found that it was only slightly damaged.

I told the emperor that good fortune had thrown this boat in my path to help me return to my native country. I asked his help in providing the materials to fix it, along with his permission to leave, both of which he was pleased to grant me.

In the meanwhile, a group of Lilliputians had been sent along with a copy of the articles drawn up against me. They made clear to the monarch of Blefuscu of the great mercy of their master and said that I would be declared a traitor if I did not return. In order to keep the peace, the emperor of Blefuscu was strongly urged to have me sent back to Lilliput, bound hand and foot.

The emperor of Blefuscu denied this request. Instead he offered me his full protection if I would remain in his service. I believed him to be sincere, but told him that I would rather risk myself in the ocean than be a cause of fighting between two great rulers.

With the help of five hundred of His Majesty's workmen, I set to work on the boat. I fashioned two sails by quilting together thirteen sheets of their strongest linen. A great stone served as my anchor, and some of their largest trees were cut down in order to make oars and masts. In about a month, the work was done and I was ready to leave.

At the emperor's command, my ship was supplied with the food, water, several purses of gold coins, and a life-size picture of himself, which I put in one of my gloves to keep it from being damaged. I also took six cows and two bulls, hoping to continue the breed back at home.

I set sail on the twenty-fourth of September, 1701, at six in the morning. It was two days before I spotted a sail steering to the southeast of me. Between five and six that evening I caught up to her. My heart leaped to see that she was flying English colors.

The vessel was a merchant ship returning from Japan. The captain was a civil man and an excellent sailor. Still, when I told him who I was, and where I had been, the captain thought me mad. When I showed him the cows and bulls, however, along with the emperor of Blefuscu's picture, he was truly amazed.

I returned home in April of 1702. I remained there for two months with my wife and family, but my desire to travel would not allow me to stay any longer.

PART II:
A VOYAGE TO BRODDINGDANG

CHAPTER 1

A great storm is described. The author
goes to fetch water and is left on shore, where he
is taken by one of the natives.

∽

Having been sentenced by nature and fortune to a restless life, I again left my native country. I took leave of my wife and children and went on board the *Adventure,* a merchant ship commanded by Captain John Nicholas.

We left on the twentieth day of June, 1702. Very strong winds carried us around the Cape of Good Hope and through to the Straits of Madagascar.

On the nineteenth of April, a storm moved in, driving us to the east of the Molucca Islands. The storm lasted for twenty days and we were carried about five hundred leagues to the east. Our supplies held out, although we had very little water.

On the sixteenth day of June, we came in full view of a great land mass. On the south side was a small neck of land with a shallow creek jutting into the sea. We cast anchor close by and our captain sent a dozen of his men in search of water. I joined this party, curious to see this unknown country.

While the rest of the men wandered on the shore to find some water, I walked alone in the other direction. There was nothing to see but barren, rocky land, so I turned back toward the creek. There I was alarmed to see our men already in the boat and rowing to the ship with great speed. A huge creature was walking into the sea after them. The water came only to his knees and he took very long steps. Our men had a good lead on him, though, and the monster was unable to catch them.

I ran away as fast as I could. I climbed up a steep hill, which gave me a good view of the country. I was surprised at the length of the grass, which in those grounds was more than twenty feet high. I spotted a wide road and walked on it for some time, unable to see much past the corn rising at least forty feet on either side of me. At the end of an hour I reached a series of steps that passed from this field into the next field, but each step was six feet high and I could not climb them.

I was looking for a gap in the stones when one of the creatures in the next field began coming toward me. He was as tall as the one I had seen in the sea and covered about ten yards with every step he took. At the top of the stairs he stopped and called out in a voice so loud and booming that I initially mistook it for thunder.

Seven more of these monsters came running, each with reaping hooks in their hands. These people were not as well dressed as the first and I assumed that they were servants or laborers. The first man spoke to the servants for a while and they went off to reap the corn in the field where I was hiding. I kept away from them as well as I could. The stalks of corn were sometimes less than a foot apart, though, and it was very hard to squeeze between them. Also, the jagged ends of the fallen ears were stiff and sharp. They easily cut through my clothes and my flesh.

The reapers had come within a hundred yards of me and I was exhausted. I lay down, wishing to die, and regretted my foolishness in attempting a second voyage against all advice. I couldn't help but think of Lilliput, whose inhabitants looked upon me as a giant. How small one Lilliputian would appear among these creatures.

One of the reapers was within ten yards of me now. With the next step I would be squashed to death under his foot or cut in two with his reaping hook. I screamed as loud as fear could make

me and the creature stopped short, looking around for some time until he saw me lying on the ground.

He studied me for a while before taking me up between his forefinger and his thumb and bringing me close to his eyes. I was fearful every moment that he would drop me on the ground and could not stop myself from shedding tears. I turned my head to one side, trying to let him know how much the pressure of his fingers was hurting me. He seemed to understand and placed me into his coat pocket before running along to his master.

This was the head farmer I had seen before. I watched from the coat pocket as his servant explained how he had found me. Lifting me out of his pocket, he placed me on my hands and knees upon the ground. I immediately stood up and walked slowly backward and forward, to show I had no intention of running. They sat down around me. I pulled off my hat and made a long bow to the farmer. I fell on my knees and lifted my hands, pleading with him as loudly as I could.

The farmer spoke to me often and I answered as loudly as I could in several languages. He laid his ear within two yards of me, but it was all in vain. We could not understand each other. He sent his servants back to work. Taking his handkerchief out of his pocket, he folded it in two and placed it flat on the ground, making a sign for me to step into it. For fear of falling, I laid myself at full length upon the handkerchief. He carried me home in this manner to show me to his wife. At first she ran away, as one would do at the sight of a spider or a rat, but she soon saw how I behaved myself and later grew extremely caring toward me.

Lunch was served and the rest of the family came to the table, including the wife, three children, and an old grandmother. It was a big meat dish, about four feet by twenty feet in size. The farmer placed me at some distance from him on the table, which was about thirty feet from the ground. I kept as far as I could from the edge, being terribly afraid of falling.

With his meal finished, the master went back out to his servants. The wife was put in charge of me, and she put me on her bed to get some rest. I slept for about two hours, dreaming I was at home with my wife and children, but waking to find myself alone in a room about three hundred feet wide and over two hundred feet high. The bed I was in was about eight yards from the floor. I was considering how to get off it when two large rats crept up the curtains and leaped toward me.

I rose in a fright and drew my long knife. These horrible animals attacked me from both sides, but I managed to kill one. At the sight of this, the second ran off. After this adventure, I walked to and fro on the bed trying to recover my breath and raise my spirits. These creatures were the size of a large dog. I measured the tail of the dead rat and found it to be two yards long.

Soon after, my mistress came into the room. Finding me all bloody, she ran and took me up in her hand. I pointed to the dead rat, making signs to show her that I wasn't hurt. She set me on a table and wiped some of the blood from me. I showed her my bloody knife, which she wiped clean as well. The maid was called and, taking the dead rat up with a pair of tongs, she threw it out the window.

CHAPTER 2

*A description of the farmer's daughter. The author is
carried into town and then to the city.*

෴

My mistress had a daughter of nine years old
and she fixed up her doll's cradle for me to sleep
in. The cradle was put into a small drawer of a cabinet and the cabinet was placed upon a hanging
shelf for fear of rats. This was my bed all the time I
stayed with those people.

This young girl was so handy that she soon
made me seven shirts and some other linens. She
was also my teacher. When I pointed to anything,
she told me the name of it in her own language.
In a few days, I was able to call for whatever I had

a mind to. She gave me the name Gildrig, meaning "mannequin," which the family took up, and afterward the whole kingdom. I called her Glumdalclitch, which meant "little nurse."

My master had an idea about how to make money off of me. He carried me to the market day in the next town in a box, bringing my nurse along as well. My box was closed on every side, with holes to let in air and a little door for me to go in and out of. The girl had been careful to put the quilt of her doll's bed into it, but I was still terribly shaken about in the journey.

We stopped first at a local inn. After talking with the inn-keeper, my master gave notice through the town of a strange creature to be seen who was like a miniature human and could perform a hundred tricks. That night, I was placed upon a table in the largest room of the inn. My master would only allow thirty people at a time to see me as I walked about on the table. After paying my respects in their language, I made a toast to their health, drew out my knife, and waved it around it like a master fencer.

I was shown that day to twelve sets of people, doing the same routine over and over. By the end of the day I was half dead with weariness and anger. My master gave public notice that he would show me again at the next market day.

My master soon found that he could make quite a bit of money by showing me, and decided to carry me to the largest cities of the kingdom. We set out for a city near the middle of the empire, some three thousand miles away from our house. Glumdalclitch carried me the whole way in a box tied about her waist. She had lined the box on all sides with the softest cloth she could get and made it as comfortable as possible. We were ten weeks into our journey and I had been shown in eighteen large towns along the way, besides many villages and private families.

On the twenty-sixth of October, we arrived at the city. My master rented a large room and I was shown ten times a day to the wonder and satisfaction of all the people. I could now speak the language fairly well, and understood every word that was said to me.

The more money my master made, the more he wanted. Meanwhile, I had quite lost my appetite and was nearly reduced to a skeleton. By the time a gentleman came from the court, commanding my master to bring me there for the queen's entertainment, the farmer already thought that I would die soon

Her Majesty was much delighted with my performance. I fell on my knees and begged the honor of kissing her foot, but she offered instead her little finger, which I hugged with both my arms. She asked me questions about my country and my travels, which I answered as clearly as I could. She then asked my master if he was willing to sell me for a good price. Thinking I could not live another month, he was happy enough to part with me and asked for one thousand pieces of gold. These were ordered for him on the spot.

I then turned to the queen and asked, since I was now Her Majesty's most humble creature, if Glumdalclitch might be allowed to stay and continue to be my nurse and teacher. Her Majesty agreed to this and easily got the farmer's consent, as he was eager to have his daughter favored at court. The farmer left, bidding me farewell. I did not say a word in reply.

CHAPTER 3

The author is presented to the king.
An apartment is provided for him, and he fights
with the queen's dwarf.

∽

The king was an educated person, and was especially fond of mathematics. When he observed my shape and saw me walking around, he wondered if I was not a machine built by some creative artist. When he heard my voice, though, he could not hide his amazement.

Three scholars were called for. These gentlemen examined me in great detail. They all agreed that I could not have been made according to the laws of nature. I was too small and too slow to avoid most dangers, and they could not think of a single animal that wouldn't beat me. One of them thought I was a baby, but this idea was rejected as my body was fully formed and my beard showed my age. They did not think that I was a dwarf, as the queen's dwarf, who was the smallest ever known, was some thirty feet tall. After much debate, they agreed that I was a freak of nature.

I assured His Majesty that I came from a country where there were millions of both sexes just like me, along with animals, trees, and houses that were all appropriate for our size, but he did not believe me. He and the queen ordered that I be taken good care of and that Glumdalclitch tend to me.

The queen commanded her cabinetmaker to make a box that might serve as my bedroom. After three weeks, he had built a fine box sixteen feet square and twelve feet high with curtained windows, a door, two closets, and a proper bed.

The board that made the ceiling was hinged so that Glumdalclitch could remove my tiny bed when she needed to wash the sheets. My room was quilted on all sides, including the floor and ceiling, to prevent any accidents from the damage done by those who carried me.

The queen became quite fond of me. She had a set of clothes made for me in the fashion of the kingdom, and she never dined without me. I had a table placed upon the one at which she ate, just at her left elbow, and a chair to sit on. I had a complete set of plates and silverware made for me, not much bigger than what I'd seen made for the furniture of a doll's house. Her Majesty would put a bit of her meat upon one of my dishes. I carved a bit for myself and she was amused to watch me eat in miniature. For my part, it made me rather sick to watch her eat. She took up in one mouthful as much as a dozen English farmers could eat at one meal.

Nothing angered and embarrassed me as much as the queen's dwarf who, being of the lowest ranking that ever was in the country, became so proud at seeing a creature so much beneath him that he would always show off and try to look big as he passed me.

One day at dinner, this cruel little creature was so annoyed by something I had said that he picked me up, dropped me into a large silver bowl of cream, and then ran away as fast as he could. I fell in head over heels. If I had not been a good swimmer, I might have drowned. Glumdalclitch was at the other end of the table, but she managed to come to my rescue, fishing me out before I'd swallowed more than a quart of cream.

I was put to bed, and suffered no real damage other than

the loss of a suit of clothes. The dwarf was soundly punished and forced to drink up the bowl of cream into which he had dropped me. To my great satisfaction, the queen gave him away soon after that event.

The queen frequently scolded me for my fearfulness. She used to ask me whether all the people of my kingdom were as cowardly as myself. The idea that I was a coward was mostly due to my fear of flies. Each of these was as large as a pigeon, and I had much trouble defending myself against them. Often, I would cut them in pieces with my knife as they flew past me. My skill at this feat was greatly admired.

I had another opportunity to demonstrate my courage. One morning Glumdalclitch set my box upon a window, as she usually did on fair days to give me air. I had opened my curtains and was sitting down at my table to eat a piece of sweet-cake when about twenty wasps came into my room, humming louder than two dozen bag-pipes. Some of them took my cake. Others flew about my head, making me afraid of their stings.

I stood up and used my knife to kill four of the monsters, although the rest got away. I took out their stings and found them to be at least an inch and a half long and as sharp as needles. I kept all of these and have since shown them, with some other curiosities, in several parts of Europe.

CHAPTER 4

The author's way of traveling. Several adventures that happened to him.

⌒

Besides the box in which I was usually carried, the queen ordered a smaller one to be made for me that would more easily fit into Glumdalclitch's lap. This traveling closet was about twelve feet square, with a window in the middle of three of the sides. Each window was covered with iron wire to prevent accidents. On the fourth side, two strong staples were fixed so that the person carrying me could attach the box to his or her belt. I had a closet in this box and a hammock hung from the ceiling. The box also had two chairs and a table, all screwed to the floor.

A coach was allowed to Glumdalclitch and me, in which her governess often took her out to see the town or go to the shops. I was always carried in my box, though my nurse would often take me out and place me in her hand so that I could more easily see the houses and people as we passed along the streets.

I may have lived happily enough in that country, if my smallness had not led to several ridiculous and troublesome accidents. The greatest danger I faced there was from a monkey who belonged to one of the kitchen clerks.

Glumdalclitch had locked me in her room while she went somewhere on a visit. The weather was very warm and the windows to Glumdalclitch's room had been left open, as well as the windows and the door of my bigger box, in which I usually lived. As I sat at my table, I heard

something bounce in at the window. I was star-
tled, and I looked out my window and saw the
animal jumping about. He leaped up and down
until he came to my box. After some time peep-
ing and grinning in all of the windows, he spied
me and reached one of his paws in the door as a
cat does with a mouse.

I did my best to avoid him, but he grabbed the
end of my coat and dragged me out. He held me
as a nurse does a child. When I tried to struggle he
squeezed me so hard that I thought it best to sur-
render. He held me in this way for a while,
stroking me as if I were one of his children, until
there was a noise at the door. Suddenly, he leaped
out of the window, still holding me in his paw,
and clambered up onto the roof.

Soon, half of the palace was in an uproar. The
servants ran for ladders and the monkey was
seen by hundreds, sitting upon the edge of the
building, holding me like a baby in one of his

forepaws. He crammed into my mouth some left-over food he had stolen from the kitchen and patted me when I would not eat. Many of the people below were laughing. I cannot truly blame them, as the sight was surely funny to everyone but myself.

The ladders were set up on all sides now. The monkey saw himself surrounded and, not being able to get away without the use of all four paws, he dropped me on the ledge and ran off. I sat there for a while, five hundred yards from the ground, expecting every moment to be blown off the roof to my death. Finally, one of the servants reached me.

I almost choked to death on the filthy stuff the monkey had crammed down my mouth, but my dear little nurse picked it out of my mouth with a small needle. Still, I was so sick and bruised that I kept to my bed for a week. The king, queen, and all of the court asked about my health daily, and the monkey was sent away, with orders that no such animal be kept around the palace.

Later, I visited the king. He asked me what my thoughts were while I lay in the monkey's paw. He wanted to know what I would have done had something similar happened in my own country.

I told His Majesty that in Europe we had no monkeys, except ones that were so small that I could deal with a dozen of them together if they attacked me. As for that animal who had carried me away, which was indeed as large as an elephant, I told the King that if I had been able to make use of my knife I might have given him such a wound when he poked his paw into my chamber as to make him remove it faster than he had put it in.

I spoke these words as bravely as I could, but the response was nothing but laughter.

CHAPTER 5

*The king and queen travel to distant frontiers.
The author joins them. The way in which he leaves
the country and returns to England.*

⁓

I had a strong desire to at some time recover my freedom, but it was impossible to imagine by what means. The ship in which I sailed was the first of its kind known within those parts. The king had given strict orders that if another appeared, it should be taken ashore and all of its passengers should be brought in a cart to the city. He wanted to get me a woman to start a family with.

I would rather have died than have undergone the disgrace of having my family line kept in cages like tamed canaries and, perhaps in time, sold about the kingdom. I was treated well by the king and queen. Still, I could never forget my own family back home. I longed to be among them, and to walk about the streets and fields without fear of being stepped on..

I had been two years in this country when Glumdalclitch and I joined the king and queen on a journey to the south coast of the kingdom. As usual, I was carried in my traveling box. By the time we got to the end of our journey, my nurse and I were very tired. I had gotten a small cold, but Glumdalclitch was so ill that she had to be kept in her bedroom.

I wished to see the ocean, which was the only possible means for my escape, and pretended to be sicker than I really was. I begged to take in the fresh air of the sea with a page of whom I was quite fond. I shall never forget with what unwillingness my nurse agreed, nor the strict orders she gave the page to take care of me. At the same time, she burst into a flood of tears, as if she had some idea of what was to happen.

The boy took me out in my box about half an hour's walk from the palace. I ordered him to set me down and, parting one of my curtains, cast many a sad look toward the sea. I found myself not well and told the page that I wished to take a nap in my hammock. He shut the window to keep out the cold and I soon fell asleep.

I found myself suddenly awoken by a violent pull upon the ring which fastened at the top of my box. I felt the box raised up high in the air and carried quickly forward. The first jolt nearly shook me out of my hammock and I called out several times, as loudly as I could, but to no purpose.

I looked toward my windows and could see nothing but clouds and sky. There was a noise just over my head like the flapping of wings and I began to understand. Some eagle had gotten hold of my box by his beak with the intention of letting it fall on a rock, like a tortoise in a shell, and then eating whatever was inside.

In a little time, the noise and flutter of the wings increased and I felt my box being tossed up and down like a signpost on a windy day. I felt many bangs and bounces and then, all of a sudden, felt myself falling straight down at a frightening speed. My fall was stopped by a terrible squash, which sounded louder to my ears than the Niagara Falls. After that, I laid in the dark for another minute before my box rose so high that I could see light from the tops of the windows.

I now realized that I had fallen into the sea. My box, because of my weight and the weight of my belongings, floated about five feet deep in the water. Every joint of my box was well grooved. The door did not move on hinges, but slid up and down, which kept the seal tight so that very little water came in. I was able to slide open the door on the roof slightly to let in enough air to breathe. Still, a break in just one pane of glass would have meant immediate death and I watched nervously as the water oozed in at several crannies.

How often did I then wish myself with my dear Glumdalclitch, from whom one single hour had divided me! I may also say, in the midst of my bad luck, that I could not but think of the grief she would suffer for my loss, the displeasure of the queen, and the ruin of her fortune.

Being in this sad state, I was alarmed to hear some kind of grating noise at the back of my box where the staples were fastened. Soon after, I began to imagine that the box was being pulled or towed along in the sea. I unscrewed one of my chairs and, placing it directly under the roof door, called for help in as loud a voice as I could manage. I then fastened my handkerchief to a stick and thrust it through the hole, waving it several times in the air.

I found no effect from all of this, but I knew that I was being towed somehow and, in the space of an hour, felt the back of my box strike against something hard. I heard a noise, like that of a cable grating as it passed through a ring, and found my box raised up by at least three feet. At this, I waved my handkerchief through the opening again and shouted out until I was hoarse. In return I heard a great shout repeated three times, which caused me such joy as cannot be understood by those who have not felt it. There was a loud noise overhead and somebody called through the hole in English: *"If there be anybody below, let him speak."*

I answered that I was an Englishman and begged to be delivered out of my dungeon. The voice replied that I was safely fastened to their ship and that the carpenter would soon come and saw a hole in the cover large enough to pull me out.

After they had freed me, the sailors wanted to ask me a thousand questions. But the captain saw that I was ready to faint and took me into his cabin to rest. Before I went to sleep, I let him know that I had some furniture in my box that was too valuable to be lost, including a fine hammock, two chairs, a table, and a cabinet. The captain thought that I was mad but promised to do as I asked, upon which the crew found all of the objects that I had described.

I slept for many hours, but I was disturbed by dreams of the place I had left and the dangers I had escaped. When I awoke the captain ordered supper immediately. He entertained me with great kindness and asked that I tell him about my travels. He told me of his fear that my brain was disturbed, or that I had been punished at the command of some prince.

I begged his patience to hear me tell my story, which I did faithfully, from the time I left England to the moment he discovered me. To further confirm what I said, I asked him to have my cabinet brought forth. From this I brought forth certain rarities I had saved, including some hairs I had rescued from the king's shavings and fashioned into a comb, pins and needles from a foot to half a yard long, four wasps' stings, and a gold ring the queen had once given me from her own little finger.

The captain was amazed by my story, but he wondered whether the king or queen of that country were hard of hearing, which caused me to speak as loudly as I did. It took me some time to cure myself of the habit of shouting.

The captain was on his way back to England, although we called on one or two ports along the way. I did not leave the ship until we came back to my homeland on the third day of June, 1706.

As I rode home, seeing the smallness of the houses, the trees, the cattle, and the people, I began to think myself in Lilliput. I was afraid of crushing every traveler I met and often called aloud to have them stand out of the way, so that I nearly ended up with one or two broken heads for my arrogance.

When I came to my own house, I bent down to go in the door, for fear of striking my head. My wife ran to embrace me, but I stooped lower than her knees. My daughter kneeled to ask my blessing, but I could not see her until she stood up. Because of my behavior, my whole family was of the opinion that I had lost my mind.

My family and I soon came to an understanding, although my wife made me promise that I would never go to sea again. I agreed readily, but my evil destiny ordered otherwise.

PART III: A VOYAGE TO LAPUTA, BALNIBARBI, GLUBBDUBDRIB, LUGGNAGG, AND JAPAN

CHAPTER 1

The author sets out on his third voyage.
He is taken by pirates. He arrives at an island and
is received onto Laputa.

✺

I had not been at home for more than ten days when Captain William Robinson, Commander of the *Hopewell,* came to my house and invited me to be the surgeon of a ship on a voyage to the East Indies. He offered to pay me double my usual salary. The thirst I had to see the world continued to be as strong as ever. The only difficulty lay in persuading my wife, whose permission I at last received.

We set out the fifth day of August, 1706, and sailed on to Tonquin, where the captain planned to stay for some time. Some of the goods he planned to buy were not yet ready so the captain decided to do some trading in the nearby islands. He bought a small one-masted boat called a sloop, loaded it with several goods the Tonquinese preferred, staffed it with fourteen men, and appointed me master of the sloop.

We had not sailed three days when two pirate ships overtook us. Both ships boarded us at the same time and, ill-equipped to defend ourselves, we fell down, kneeling and touching our faces to the deck. The pirates tied us with strong ropes and set guards upon us while they searched the boat.

Afterward, the pirates divided my men equally among the ships to be put to work as slaves and I was set adrift in a small canoe with paddles, a sail, and four days' supplies.

When the pirates had left, I discovered some islands to the southeast. I set up my sail with a plan to reach the nearest of the islands, which I accomplished in about three hours. The island was mostly rocky. Only a little piece of it had tufts of grass and sweet smelling herbs. I took out my supplies and, after refreshing myself, hid the rest in a cave, of which there were many. I gathered plenty of eggs upon these rocks and then lay all the night in the cave.

I slept very little, kept awake by my thoughts. I considered how impossible it was to survive in such a place and how miserable my end would be. I was so upset that by the time I had the spirit to creep out of my cave, the day had grown late. I walked awhile along the rocks. The sky was perfectly clear. The sun was so hot I had to turn my face from it.

Suddenly the bright sun was obscured. Turning back, I saw a vast, solid body between me and the sun. The body was moving toward the island. It seemed to be about two miles high and it hid the sun for six minutes. It appeared to be of a firm substance, the bottom flat and smooth and shining brightly from the reflection of the sea below. I took my pocket glass out and could plainly see a great number of people moving up and down the sides of it, though what those people were doing I could not tell.

The reader can hardly imagine my amazement at seeing this island in the air, inhabited by men who were able (it seemed) to raise, sink, or put the island into motion as they saw fit. I soon saw that the island was coming closer. As it neared me I could see that every side of it was covered with galleries and staircases, one leading to the other. On the lowest level I saw some people fishing. I waved my cap and my handkerchief at the island. As it got even nearer, I shouted as loudly as I could.

A crowd had gathered on the side and I saw that they were pointing at me, although they did not shout back. The number of people in the crowd increased and the island was raised in such a manner that the lowest level appeared less than a hundred yards away from where I stood.

At length, the flying island was raised to a convenient height above me and a chain was let down from the lowest level with a seat fastened to the bottom. I sat myself upon it and was drawn up by pulleys.

CHAPTER 2

*The humors and behaviors of the Laputans. The author's
receptions there, and the inhabitants' fears.*

∽

After boarding the vessel, I was surrounded by
a crowd of people. They looked on me with great
wonder and I stared at them in much the same
way. Their heads were all bent to the right or left,
with one of their eyes turned inward and the
other turned directly up to the heavens. Their
clothes were covered with symbols of the moon,
sun, and stars, along with many musical instruments. Many had the appearance of servants,
holding pouches fastened to the end of sticks. In
each of these pouches was a small quantity of

dried peas. With these devices, the servants now and then tapped the mouths and ears of the person who stood near them.

It turned out that the minds of these people were so full of their own thoughts that they could neither speak nor listen to the conversation of others without being reminded to do so. For that reason, those who could afford it always employed a servant known as a flapper. When two or more people were in company, it was the job of the flapper to strike the mouth of the person who was to speak and the right ear of the person who was to listen. The flapper also joined the master on all of his walks, giving him the occasional flap on his eyes. Without this, the master would be so wrapped up in his own thoughts that he would constantly be falling and bumping into things.

While we were climbing the stairs to the top of the island, the people leading me often times forgot what they were doing until they were reminded by their flappers. At last we entered the palace and proceeded into the main chamber. I saw the king seated on his throne, attended on both sides by noble lords. Before the throne was a large table filled with globes, spheres, and mathematical instruments.

The king was deep in thought about a problem and we stood there for an hour or so while he solved it. Finally, looking toward me and the company I was in, he remembered my arrival, which he had been told about several times.

As he spoke to me, a young man came up and flapped me gently on the right ear. I made signs as well as I could that I had no use for such a reminder. I later found out that this gave His Majesty, and the whole court, a very low opinion of my intelligence. The king asked me several questions. When it was clear that neither of us could understand the other, I was led away to a comfortable apartment.

Dinner was brought to me, and four lords did me the honor of dining with me. We had several courses, including a shoulder of lamb cut into triangles, a piece of beef cut into rhombuses, and a pudding formed in the shape of a cylinder. There was also a slice of duck tied up to look like a fiddle and various sausages twisted into the shapes of flutes and harps. While we ate I asked the names of several things in their language, and I was soon able to call for more bread or drink.

After dinner, my company left and a teacher was sent to me by the king's order, along with a flapper. He brought with him a pen, ink, paper, and three or four books. We sat together for hours. He showed me the figures of the sun, moon, and stars. He gave me the names and descriptions of all the musical instruments, as well as the general terms for playing on each of them.

After he left, I placed all the words he had taught me in alphabetical order. Following this method and memorizing the lists that I made, I had some understanding of their language in just a few days. One of the first words I mastered was the term for their flying island: Laputa.

The king also ordered a tailor to come and measure me for a new suit of clothes. This man worked very differently from the tailors I was used to, taking his measurements with a ruler and compass and graphing the results on paper. The clothes he made fit me quite poorly. I was told this was due to a mistake in the calculations, a frequent event regarded with little importance.

As we traveled, the island stopped over certain towns and villages so that the king could receive the requests of his subjects. Several threads were let down with small weights attached to them. The people strung their requests to these threads and sent them back up. We also received food and water from below by way of pulleys.

I soon learned that, on account of their many fears, these poor people never enjoyed a minute's peace. For example, they worried that the earth, by the continuous approach of the sun toward it, must in time be swallowed up. They also worried that the earth, having recently escaped collision with a comet that would have destroyed it, would certainly collide with the next comet. They calculated that this comet would arrive in 130 years. When they met in the morning, their first question was about the sun's health, how it looked at its rising and setting, and what hopes there were of it avoiding the approaching comet.

CHAPTER 3

The secret of the flying island.
The author grows restless.

ᴄᴏ

The flying island was exactly circular. It measured four and a half miles around and contained four thousand acres of land. The bottom of the island was made of polished steel and the roofs of the buildings declined so that all the rain and dew that fell on the island drained to the center, where it was emptied into four large basins. The ruler had the ability to raise and lower the island above the clouds to control the amount of water in the basins.

At the center of the island was a large pit known as the Astronomer's Face. The greatest curiosity here, and one on which the fate of the island depends, is a great magnet, six yards long and three yards across at its thickest. The magnet is held up by a rod of steel that passes through the middle and is placed in a way that even the weakest hand can turn it. The stone is surrounded by a cylinder of steel. The cylinder is anchored in the steel at the bottom of the island, and the stone cannot be moved.

The island is made to rise, fall, and move from one place to another by means of this magnet. The island moves down when the magnet is vertical, with its attracting end toward the earth. When the repelling end points downward, the island moves directly upward. By slanting the stone at different angles, the island can be moved from side to side. When the stone is exactly parallel with the horizon, the island stands still. The magnetic pull of the stone is tied to the earth below so that the king cannot move beyond the borders of his land, nor can he rise above the height of four miles.

Although I cannot say that I was ill-treated on this island, I must confess that I wished to leave it. Neither prince nor people appeared to be curious about anything except for mathematics and music, subjects of which I knew very little. The people there were so involved in their own thoughts that I never met with less agreeable companions.

I asked the king for permission to depart and he granted it to me easily. On the sixteenth of February, I left His Majesty and the court. The king gave me the name of a friend of his in Lagado, the capital city, and a note to give to his friend. By the time I was let down from the lowest level of the island, I was about two miles from the city.

CHAPTER 4

The author leaves Laputa. He descends to
Balnibarbi and arrives at the city of Lagado. The author
is well received by a great lord.

❧

I felt some satisfaction at finding myself on firm ground again. I walked to the city of Lagado with no concern, being dressed like a native and able to speak with them quite easily. I soon found the house of the person to whom the King had sent me, presented my letter, and was received with much kindness.

The great lord, whose name was Munodi, ordered me an apartment in his own house, where I stayed during my visit. The next morning he took me in his chariot to see the town, which was about half the size of London. The houses were very strangely built and most of them looked in need of repair. The people in the streets walked fast and looked wild. Their clothing was usually nothing but rags.

We traveled about three miles into the country. There were many laborers working with several sorts of tools in the ground, but I was not able to figure out what they were doing. No grass or corn was growing, although the soil appeared to be excellent.

I asked my host to explain what could be meant by so many busy hands and heads, as I could not discover what they were accomplishing. I had never seen soil so unused, houses so poorly built, or a people whose expression showed so much unhappiness.

Lord Munodi was highly respected and had been the Governor of Lagado for many years. He made no answer to my question, but when we returned to his palace he asked me what I thought of his building and his appearance. Everything about him was regular and polite, which I did not hesitate to tell him. He then told me that if I would go with him to his country house some twenty miles away, we could more freely discuss my question. I happily agreed.

In three hours traveling, the scene was wholly changed. There were neatly built houses surrounded by fields, meadows, and vineyards. His Excellency told me that this was where his estate began and that his countrymen laughed at him for setting so poor an example for the kingdom.

We came at length to his house, which was built according to the best rules of ancient architecture. I praised everything I saw. After dinner he told me that he would probably soon have to tear down his houses both in town and in the countryside in order to rebuild them in the present style. He would have to destroy all his plantations and give the same directions to his tenants, or else be humiliated and perhaps even anger the king.

Apparently, some forty years ago a group of people had gone to Laputa. They had returned five months later with some small knowledge of mathematics. These people immediately shared their new ideas about the arts, sciences, languages, and mechanics. They created a great academy of projectors in Lagado, which had proven so popular that now every town has such an academy.

In these colleges, professors dreamed up new rules and methods of farming and building, as well as new instruments and tools for all trades. It was their hope that one day a single man would be able to do the work of ten, a palace could be built in a week, and tools could be made so durable that they would never need to be repaired. All the fruits of the earth would ripen when the people wished it, and a number of other happy proposals will be realized.

The only problem was that none of these projects had actually worked yet. In the meantime, the country lay wasted, the houses were in ruins, and the people were without food and clothes. Rather than being discouraged, the planners were fifty times more determined to promote their mad schemes.

Lord Munodi said he would be happy to show me the Grand Academy. After listening to his story and seeing the state of the things around me, I felt that such a visit would profit me little.

CHAPTER 5

The author leaves Lagado, arriving at Maldonada.
No ship is ready and he takes a short voyage.

౧

T he continent of which this kingdom is a part
extends itself, as I have reason to believe, eastward
to that unknown part of America west of
California and north of the Pacific Ocean. There
is a busy port. Much trading is done with the
island of Luggnagg, which is situated to the
north-west. This island is only about a hundred
leagues away from Japan, so I planned to direct
my travels this way in order to return to Europe.

When I arrived at the port of Maldonada there
was no ship in the harbor bound for Luggnagg,

nor likely to be one for some time. A noble gentleman suggested that since the ships bound for Luggnagg could not be ready in less than a month, it might be agreeable for me to visit the island of Glubbdubdrib, about five leagues to the south-west. At his recommendation, I set off for Glubbdubdrib with a few traveling companions.

Glubbdubdrib, as nearly as I can interpret the word, means the island of sorcerers or magicians. It is a small island governed by the head of a tribe of magicians. The governor and his family have servants who are somewhat unusual. By his skill in sorcery, he has the power to call forth whomever he pleases from the dead to be in his service for twenty-four hours. He cannot, however, call forth the same person twice within a three month period, except upon very unusual circumstances.

My two traveling companions and I entered the gate of the palace between two rows of guards who were armed and dressed in a very strange manner. Something in their expression made my flesh creep with a horror I cannot express. We passed through several apartments until we came to the main chamber, where we were permitted to sit on three stools near the lowest step of His Majesty's throne.

His Majesty understood the language of Balnibarbi, though it was different from his own, and he wished me to give him some account of my travels. He dismissed all of his attendants with a turn of the finger. To my great amazement, they disappeared in an instant, like visions in a dream when you are suddenly awakened. It was difficult to recover from this sight, but His Majesty assured me that no harm would come to me.

We stayed on the island for ten days, spending most of every day with His Majesty. I soon grew so familiar with the sight of spirits that they gave me no fear at all after their third or fourth appearance. A great curiosity had replaced my fear and His Highness let me summon the spirits of whomever I chose. I was told that I could ask the spirits any question I wished and they would answer me truthfully, as lying was a talent of no use in the lower world.

I wished to see Alexander the Great, and he was called into the room and answered all of my questions. I next called forth Julius Caesar and Brutus. I observed with much pleasure that they were on good terms. It would be boring to trouble the reader with the vast number of people whom I called up. I mainly fed my eyes with the destroyers of tyrants and the restorers of freedom to injured countries, but it is impossible to express the satisfaction I received from their visits.

CHAPTER 6

The author's return to Maldonada.
He sails to the kingdom of Luggnagg.

⌒

The day of our departure came. I took leave of His Highness and returned with my two companions to Maldonada, where a ship was ready to sail for Luggnagg. On the twenty-first of April, 1708, we sailed into the river of Clumegnig, which is a seaport town at the south-east point of the island off Luggnagg.

The customs officer spoke to me in Balnibarbian and I gave him a short account of my history, trying to make my story as believable as possible. I said that I was Dutch, as my plan was to get to Japan and I knew the Dutch were the only foreigners allowed entry into that kingdom. The officer said that I must be locked up until he could receive orders from the court, for which he would write immediately. While I waited, I was taken to a small room with a guard placed at the door.

The note from the court arrived in two weeks and contained an order to bring me and my party to the capital city. A messenger was sent a half day's journey before us, asking His Majesty to determine the exact day and hour that I might have the honor to "lick the dust before his footstool."

I soon found this to be more than just an expression. Upon my arrival, I was told to crawl toward the king on my belly, licking the floor as I advanced. Because I was a stranger, care was taken to have the floor cleaned so that the dust would not be offensive. This mercy was usually allowed only to people of the highest rank. For one who is considered a powerful enemy of the court, the floor is often sprinkled with dust on purpose. I have even seen a great lord with his mouth so full of dust that he was unable to speak by the time he reached the throne. There was no solution to this problem either, as it is a capital offense for people to spit or wipe their mouths in His Majesty's presence.

I crept within four yards of the throne and raised myself gently to my knees before striking my forehead seven times against the ground and reciting the words of respect I had been taught. They were later interpreted to me as: "May your celestial Majesty out-live the sun, eleven moons and a half."

To this, the king answered: "*My tongue is in the mouth of my friend.*" After this, I was able to call for an interpreter and, through him, speak with the king. The king was delighted with my company

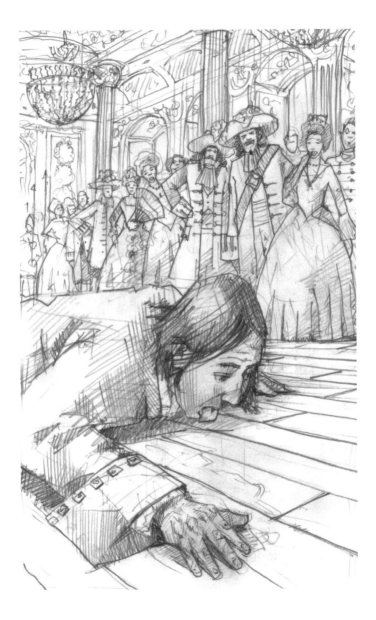

and ordered that housing be found for me at the court.

I stayed three months in this country and found the Luggnuggians to be a polite and generous people. I met many people, always attended by my interpreter, and the conversations we had were not disagreeable. One day I was asked whether or not I had seen any of their Struldbrugs, or immortals.

I said that I had not and asked what was meant by that term. I was told that sometimes a child was born with a red circular spot on the forehead, directly over the left eyebrow. This was taken as a sign that the child would never die. Their births were rare and it was believed that there were less than eleven thousand Struldbrugs of both sexes in the whole kingdom, about fifty of whom lived in the city. The births were unpredictable and purely matters of chance, as the children of the Struldbrugs themselves were usually mortal.

Upon hearing this, I was struck with a sense of incredible delight and cried out in joy. What a happy nation, where every child has at least the chance of being immortal! Happy people whose minds were free, without the weight and depression of spirit caused by the constant fear of death. I was surprised that I had not observed any of these amazing people at court. It seemed impossible that a king should not provide himself with a number of such wise and able counselors, and I was determined to give that advice to His Majesty. I was also determined to ask for the king's permission to spend the rest of my life here in conversation with these superior Struldbrugs.

The gentleman to whom I addressed these comments smiled at me, the sort of smile which usually arises from pity, and asked me what plan I should follow if I had been born a Struldbrug. I gave a long speech, answering that I could discover the difference between life and death. I could figure out all the ways to make money and become the wealthiest man in the kingdom. I would be better than all others in learning. Lastly, I would become a living source of knowledge and wisdom, and certainly become the chief advisor of the nation.

When I was done, the gentleman to whom I had been speaking said that he wished to correct me on a few mistakes I had made. He then gave me an account of the Struldbrugs among them.

He said that they commonly acted like mortals until the age of thirty years old, after which they became melancholy and dejected. When they reached the age of eighty, they suffered not only all the problems of old age, but many more that came from the dreadful idea of never dying. Overall, they were depressed, vain, incapable of friendship, and dead to all natural affection.

As soon as the Struldbrugs reach the age of eighty, they are looked on as dead in the eyes of the law. Their heirs are given their estates and a small amount is given to support them. At ninety, they usually lose their hair and teeth. Being unable to distinguish any taste, they eat whatever they can get without desire or appetite. They forget the names of things and persons, even those who are their nearest friends and relations. The language of the country changes over the years, so the Struldbrugs of one age do not understand those of another. Eventually, they are unable to speak with any of their neighbors and live in their own country as foreigners.

The Struldbrugs are hated by all sorts of people. I later saw five or six of different ages, the youngest not older than two hundred years, and they are the most horrifying sight I have ever seen. Besides the usual problems with extreme old age, they have an additional foulness that cannot be described.

My desire for never-ending life was greatly

lessened. I became ashamed of the pleasing visions I had formed and thought that no tyrant could invent a means of death I would not prefer over such a life. The king heard of all that had passed and spoke to me quite pleasantly about it. He wished that he could send a couple of Struldbrugs to my own country to arm our people against the fear of death, but it was forbidden by the laws of their country. I could not help but agree with these laws and, in fact, all of the laws of that kingdom. I even agreed with the feeling of the people about the treatment of the Struldbrugs.

※

On the sixteenth day of May, 1709, I took solemn leave of His Majesty and all my friends. In fifteen days we had completed the voyage to Japan and landed at a small port town on the south-east part of the main island. At landing, I showed the Customs House officer a letter of recommendation from the king.

I continued on to the port of Nangasac and, on the ninth day of June, 1709, fell into the company of some Dutch sailors aboard the ship named the *Amboyna,* headed to Amsterdam.

Nothing happened worth mentioning on this voyage. We sailed with a fair wind to the Cape of Good Hope, where we stayed only to take in fresh water. On the sixth day of April, we arrived safely at Amsterdam, having lost only three men to sickness. From Amsterdam, I soon set sail for England.

We landed on the tenth of April, 1710, and I saw once more my native country after an absence of five years and six months. I made my way home right away and arrived at two o'clock in the afternoon to find my wife and family in good health.

CHAPTER 1

The author sets out as the captain of a ship.
His men plot against him and set him on shore
in an unknown land.

∽

I stayed at home for about five months, in a very happy condition. If only I could have shown the good sense to stay for good. Instead, I accepted a generous offer to be the captain of a merchant ship called the *Adventure*.

We set sail on a trading mission on the ninth day of September, 1710. Several of my men died of tropical fever and I was forced to get recruits out of Barbados, finding out too late that many of them were pirates.

These scoundrels corrupted many of my men

and formed a plan to take over the ship. They did so one morning, rushing into my cabin, tying me up, and threatening to throw me overboard if I dared to move. A guard was placed at my door, and food and drink was occasionally provided. The pirates had full control of the ship.

After a few days, the pirates brought me out from my cabin and forced me into the lifeboat, allowing me no weapons but my knife. They rowed about a league and then set me down on a beach, after which they rowed off again.

I sat on the bank to rest and considered what to do next. When I was a little refreshed, I walked inland. I planned to turn myself over to the first people I should meet. I hoped to purchase my life from them if I could.

I walked for some time and, at last, I saw several animals in a field. One or two of the same kind of animal were sitting in trees. Their appearance was strange, and I lay down behind a bush to observe them better. Their heads and breasts were covered with thick hair and they had long beards like goats. There were long ridges of hair down their backs, on the backs of their legs, and all over their feet. The rest of their bodies were a dark brown color and had no hair. They had no tails, but climbed the trees using sharp, hooked claws. Upon the whole, I never saw in all my travels so disagreeable an animal.

I got up and started back toward the road only to find one of these creatures right in my way. The ugly monster lifted up his paw as if to strike me. I drew my knife and gave him a good blow with the flat side of it. The beast roared so loudly that a herd of at least forty animals came from the next field, howling and making ugly faces. I backed into the body of a tree and kept them off by waving my knife at them. Several of the beasts leaped into the tree though, and they began to throw things down and spit on me.

I was starting to feel quite worried when, suddenly, the creatures ran away as fast as they could. I looked around to see what had put them in such a fright, but saw only a gray horse walking softly through the field. The horse started a bit at the sight of me, but recovering himself came straight toward me, staring at me with wonder.

We both stood there, gazing at each other for some time. Finally I grew bold enough to reach my hand out to stroke his neck, but the animal raised up his left forefoot to brush my hand away. Then he neighed three or four times in such a pattern that I almost thought he was speaking to himself in some language.

Soon another horse came up, shorter and white colored. The two horses struck each other's right hooves before neighing several times back and forth. The gray horse rubbed my hat all around with his right fore hoof while the other horse felt the collar of my coat, showing great wonder. Upon the whole, their behavior was so orderly and thoughtful, and so amazing to me, that I decided they must be magicians who had disguised themselves.

Based on this reasoning, I addressed them, begging them to reveal themselves and explaining my sad situation. The two creatures stood silent as I spoke, seeming to listen with great attention. When I had finished, they neighed frequently toward each other. I could often make out the word *Yahoo,* which each of them repeated several times. As soon as they were silent, I pronounced it in a loud voice, imitating as best as I could the neighing of a horse.

This clearly surprised both of the horses and the gray horse quickly introduced a second word to me. This word can be translated roughly in our language as *Houyhnhnm.* I pronounced this as best as I could, though it was more difficult. Once again, both of the horses looked amazed.

After some conversation, the two horses took their leave, striking each other's hooves as they had before. The gray horse made signs that I should walk before him, and I thought it wise to obey.

CHAPTER 2

The author is taken to a house and his treatment there.

❧

After traveling about three miles, we came to a long building made of wood. The roof was low and covered with straw. I was comforted now, and took out some of the toys that travelers usually carry as presents to the natives. I hoped that these would please the people in the house and they would be encouraged to receive me kindly.

The gray horse made a sign for me to go into a large room with a smooth clay floor and a manger extending the whole length of one side. There were three nags and two mares; some of them sitting down, which quite amazed me. The horse followed me in, neighing several times at the others, who all answered back.

We walked through two rooms like this one. At the door of a third room, the gray horse signaled that I should wait. I heard him neigh three or four times in the other room. I waited to hear some answers in a human voice, but I heard none. The gray horse returned and made a sign for me to follow him into the room. I saw there only an attractive mare, a colt, and a foal, all sitting on their haunches upon mats of straw.

The mare rose from her mat and came close to me. She looked carefully at my hands and face before finally giving me a disapproving glance. She turned to the gray horse and I heard the word *Yahoo* repeated as they talked. The gray horse called to me again and I followed him first out into a kind of courtyard and then over to another building some distance away.

We entered the building and I saw three of the horrible creatures that I had met when I first landed. The beasts were feeding upon roots and the flesh of some animal. They held their food between the claws of their forefeet and tore at it with their teeth. The creatures were all tied to a beam by strong ropes fastened around their necks.

The gray horse untied the largest of these animals and the beast and I were brought close together by the horses, who kept repeating the word *Yahoo.* My horror and shock are not to be described when I saw in this disgusting animal a perfect human face.

The forepaws of the Yahoo differed from my hands in nothing but the length of the nails and the hairiness on the backs. I knew very well that our feet looked the same, although the horses did not know this because of my shoes. In fact, every part of our bodies was the same, except for the hairiness and the color. The horses could not understand my clothes, which kept them from seeing just how similar the Yahoo and I were.

The Sorrel Nag offered me a root, which I returned to his hoof as civilly as I could. He brought a piece of flesh from the Yahoo's kennel, but it smelled so offensive that I turned from it in disgust. He then offered me some hay and oats, but I shook my head to show that neither of these were food to me. I began to fear that I would starve in this country if I did not find some of my own species. As for those filthy Yahoos, the more I came near them, the more hateful they grew.

The gray horse observed my disgust and sent the Yahoo back to her kennel. He then put his fore hoof to his mouth, a gesture which surprised me, and made other signs to ask what I would eat. I was having trouble answering him until I happened to see a cow passing by and pointed at it. The horse led me back into the house and showed me a good store of milk in earthen and wooden vessels. He gave me a large bowl of it, which I drank quickly. I found myself immediately refreshed.

When evening approached, my master ordered a place for me to rest. It was only six yards from the house and separated from the stable of Yahoos. Here I got some straw and, after covering myself with my clothes, slept very soundly.

CHAPTER 3

The author studies the Houyhnhnm language.
He gives a short account of his voyage.

∽

My main goal was to learn the language which my master, his children, and every servant of his house were eager to teach me. I pointed to everything and asked the name of it. I then wrote these words down in my journal. I also worked hard to correct my bad accent. The *Houyhnhnms* pronounce through the nose or throat, and their language is more graceful than any other I know.

The curiosity of my master was so great that he spent many hours trying to teach me. He was convinced that I must be a Yahoo, but my cleanliness and good manners surprised him, for they were qualities completely opposite to those of the Yahoos. The Yahoos caused much trouble and were considered completely unteachable. My master was most confused by my clothes. He was not sure whether or not they were part of my body. He wanted to learn where I came from and how I gained the appearance of reason, and wished to hear the story from my own mouth.

The nature of my clothing was revealed by accident. One morning my master sent the Sorrel Nag for me. I was fast asleep and the cloth I used to cover me had fallen off on one side. The noise the nag made woke me quickly. He delivered his message in a shaky voice, after which he went to my master and gave a very confused account of what he'd seen.

When I went to visit my master, he told me what the servant had reported: that I was not the same thing when I slept as I appeared to be at other times. With the limited language I had learned, I told my master that those of my kind always covered their bodies in order to avoid either hot or cold weather. I offered to show him this, asking only his permission not to undress myself completely.

My master could not understand why we should hide what nature had given. He said that neither he nor his family were ashamed of their parts, but that I could do as I pleased. At this, I pulled off my shoes, socks, and pants, and let my shirt down to my waist.

My master lifted up my clothing and looked at each piece carefully. He examined my body closely, walking around me several times, and then declared me to be a perfect Yahoo. He said that I differed from most of my species only in the whiteness, the smoothness of my skin, the lack of hair on certain parts of my body, the shape and sharpness of my claws, and my habit of walking about on two feet.

I expressed my uneasiness with being called a Yahoo, an animal for which I had such a complete hatred. I begged him to stop using that word to talk about me and requested that the secret of clothing might be known to none but him. All of this he kindly agreed to, asking only that I hide nothing else from him.

After about ten weeks' time, I was finally able to understand most of my master's questions and, in another three months, I was able to give him more complete answers. I told him that I came from over the sea, from a far place populated by many of my kind. I explained that I had come in a great hollow vessel made from the bodies of trees. I also told him that my companions had forced me to land on this coast and then left me to fend for myself.

After listening to my story, he told me that I must be mistaken, or that I *said the thing which was not*, for they have no word for lying in their language. He thought it impossible that there could be a country beyond the sea, or that a group of animals such as myself could move a wooden vessel out upon the water. He was sure no Houyhnhnm could make such a vessel, and would certainly not trust a Yahoo to manage it. He asked me who made the ship and how it was possible that the Houyhnhnms of my country would leave it to their management.

I told him that I could go no further in my story unless he gave me his word that he would not be offended. He agreed and I went on, assuring him that the ship was made by creatures like myself who in all of my travels were the only rational animals I had seen. I told him that I was as surprised to see the Houyhnhnms act like rational beings as he was to find signs of reason in a Yahoo. I told him that if fortune ever restored me to my native country, my countrymen would hardly think it possible that a Houyhnhnm should be the ruling creature and the Yahoo the slave.

My master listened to me with an expression of great uneasiness. He wished to know whether we had Houyhnhnms among us, and what was their employment. I told him that we had great numbers, and that in summer they were kept in the fields, and in winter they were kept in houses with oats and hay. I begged him at this point to excuse me from speaking any further, for I was certain the account he received from me would be highly displeasing. He commanded me to go on, asking me to tell him the best and the worst.

I admitted that the Houyhnhnms among us were called horses and considered the most attractive and graceful animals we had. Then I told him that, when owned by persons of quality, they were often used for racing or drawing chariots. They were treated very well and taken good care of until they became too old or diseased. I described our manner of riding horses as well as I could, including our use of saddles, spurs, and whips. I added that we fastened plates of a hard substance called iron at the bottom of the hooves to prevent them from being broken.

My master was offended and wondered how we dared to ride on a Houyhnhnm's back, as surely the weakest servant in his house could shake off the strongest Yahoo. I answered that our horses were trained strictly from three to four years of age, and that they were disciplined if they proved ill-behaved.

It is impossible to explain his anger at our treatment of the Houyhnhnm race. He could hardly believe the account I had given him. He observed also that every animal in this country naturally hated the Yahoos. Even supposing us to have the gift of reason, he could not see how it were possible to cure the natural hatred all creatures had for us, nor could he see how we could tame animals and make them servants.

At that, he said he would debate the matter no further. He was far more curious to know my own story, the country where I was born, and the course my life had taken.

CHAPTER 4

The author tells his story and shows his great love for his natural country. His master responds.

⸙

I told my master that my birth was to honest parents on an island called England, which was as many days' journey as the strongest of his honor's servants could travel in a year. I told him that I was a surgeon, whose job it is to cure the sick and injured, but that I had largely taken to a life at sea. I also told him again of my most recent voyage and the misfortune that had come about.

My master wondered about the behavior of the men who had taken over my ship. I explained that these were desperate fellows, driven from their home countries because they were poor, or because they had committed crimes such as theft, robbery, forgery, and treason.

It took me several days' labor before my master understood what I meant. He could not understand why anyone would practice these vices. I tried to explain to him the ideas of power and riches, and the terrible effects of greed and envy. He raised his eyes in amazement. Power, government, war, law, and punishment were words that did not exist in their language, and my master found these ideas nearly impossible to understand.

The idea of war was especially troublesome to my master. He said it was good that our bodies were too small and weak to injure others too badly. I could not help smiling a little at his lack of knowledge about us. Then I gave him a description of cannons, muskets, pistols, bullets, swords, battles, sieges, and sea fights. I told him of ships sunk with a thousand men killed on each side and sad tales of stealing, burning and destroying.

I was going to continue when my master commanded me to silence, saying that my words had disturbed him more than he had thought possible. Although he hated the Yahoos, he couldn't blame them for their ugly nature. But when creatures pretending to possess reason were capable of such horror, that was something much worse.

My master sent for me one morning, after we had talked for many days. He said that he had been thinking about both my story and my people. Through my account, he found that I resembled other Yahoos in both the features of my body and in the manner of our minds. He spoke at some length then about the ugly nature of the Yahoo and how closely their behavior mirrored the stories I had told him.

These conversations had a strange effect on

me. I must confess that the many virtues of those excellent Houyhnhnms, when placed in comparison to how humans lived, had opened my eyes and caused me to see my fellow man in a very different light. My master's wise observations convinced me of a thousand faults in myself, of which I had no awareness before. I learned from his example a total hatred of all falsehood and disguise.

I had not been a year in this country before I found such a respect and affection for its inhabitants that I resolved never to return to humankind. Instead I would pass the rest of my life among these admirable Houyhnhnms. It was decided by fortune, though, my constant enemy, that such happiness should not fall to me.

CHAPTER 5

A grand debate at the General Assembly and
how it was determined.

༄

Every fourth year there is a council called by the whole Houyhnhnm nation, which continues on for five or six days. Representatives from all over attend and discuss the state of the several districts, such as whether they have too much or not enough hay, oats, cows, or Yahoos. If there is any district wanting, it is immediately satisfied by common agreement of the council.

One of these councils was held about three months before my departure. My master attended as the representative of our district. In this council an old debate was brought up again. My master, after his return, gave me a very detailed account of it.

The question to be debated was whether or not the Yahoos should be removed from the island. There were many arguments in favor of this. The Yahoos were the most filthy and deformed animal that nature had ever produced. They were also the most misbehaved. They trampled the fields and, if they were not watched carefully, would surely commit a thousand other horrors.

My master spoke up then. He said that he believed the first Yahoos had been driven here by the sea. Upon coming to land, they had retired to the mountains. Over time they had become much more savage than those of their own species in the country from which they had come. He said that he had now in his possession a wonderful Yahoo (meaning myself), which most

of them had heard of and many of them had seen.
He explained how he first found me, how my
body was covered with the skins and hairs of

other animals, and how I spoke a language of my own and had thoroughly learned their language.

He added that I had tried to convince him that Yahoos in other countries acted as the ruling animals and held the Houyhnhnms as servants. He also explained our manner of disciplining brute animals.

He said it was no shame to learn wisdom from brutes. Perhaps our forms of discipline might be practiced among the younger Yahoos to make them both more tame and more agreeable.

My master related all of this to me, though he concealed one specific fact, which related personally to myself, and of which I soon felt the unhappy effect.

In the meantime, I had settled in quite nicely. My master had ordered a room to be made for me, about six yards from the house. When my clothes were worn to rags, I made myself new ones with skins of rabbits. I resoled my shoes with wood that I cut from a tree and fitted into the existing leather. I often got honey out of hollow trees, which I mixed with my bread. All in all, I enjoyed perfect health and peace of mind.

When I thought of my friends and family, or the human race in general, I looked on them as Yahoos in shape and manner, though perhaps a bit more polite and with the gift of speech. I looked upon my hosts with such delight that I fell into imitating them. Since my return home, my friends have often told me that I trot like a horse, which I take as the highest compliment.

In the middle of this happiness, my master sent for me one morning a little earlier than usual. I saw by his expression that he was confused and unsure about how to begin speaking. After a short silence, he told me he did not know how I would take what he was going to say.

In the last general assembly, when the affair of the Yahoos had been taken up, the representatives had taken some offense at his keeping a Yahoo in his family, more like a Houyhnhnm than a brute animal.

The assembly recommended that he either employ me like the rest of my species or command me to swim back to the place from which I came. The first of these options was rejected by all of the Houyhnhnms who had seen me. As I had some basics of reason, it was to be feared that I might be able to force the other Yahoos into rebellion.

My master doubted if I could swim to another country and wished I would come up with some kind of vehicle resembling those I had described to him. He said that, for his own part, he would have been happy to keep me in his service for as long as I lived. He felt that I had done my best to cure myself of my bad habits.

I was struck with great grief and despair at my

master's words and fell into a faint by his feet. When I awoke, he told me he had thought me dead. I answered that death would have been too great a happiness and that, while I understood the council's decision, it might have been less strict.

I told him, however, that although I thought it impossible, I would try to build such a vessel as he had mentioned. Furthermore, the idea of death was the least of my worries. Supposing I should escape with my life, I could not imagine passing my days among Yahoos without returning to all of my old ways. My master made me a very gracious reply and allowed me the space of two months to finish my boat.

In about six weeks' time, I fashioned a rough sort of Indian canoe. I covered the canoe with the animal skins and stitched together my sails with the same material. I provided myself with four paddles, stocked my boat with meat, and took two jugs, one filled with milk and the other with water.

When the day had come for my departure, I took leave of my master and his family. My eyes were flowing with tears and my heart sunk with grief. His Honor was kind enough to see me off in my canoe and, before I left, I kneeled before him. He raised his hoof gently to my mouth, allowing me to kiss it. I paid my respects to the rest of the Houyhnhnms present. Then, getting into my canoe, I pushed off from shore.

CHAPTER 6

The author's dangerous voyage home.

∽

I began this desperate voyage at nine o'clock on the morning of the fifteenth of February, 1714. The wind was quite favorable. With the help of the tide, I made good speed. In half an hour, my master and his friends were almost out of sight. I often heard the Sorrel Nag crying out: *Hnuy illa nyha majah Yahoo,* or *Take care of yourself, gentle Yahoo.*

My plan was to find a small deserted island that could supply me with the necessities of life. In such solitude, I could at least enjoy my own thoughts and think with delight on the virtues of the Houyhnhnms. There would be no opportunity to return to the corrupt behavior of my own people.

In about two days' time, I arrived at the southeast point of New Zealand. I saw no natives in the place where I landed but, being unarmed, was afraid of going too far into the country. I found some shellfish on the shore and ate them raw, not daring to light a fire for fear of being discovered. I continued like this for three days.

On the fourth day, I ventured out a little too far and saw twenty or thirty natives at some height, not more than five hundred yards away. One of them spied me, and five of them chased after me.

I quickly ran to the shore and back to my canoe. Before I could get far enough out to sea, the natives fired arrows at me, one of which wounded me just inside my left knee. I was afraid this arrow might be poisoned and, after rowing safely away, I sucked the wound clean as best I could and bandaged it.

I was at a loss for what to do next. I dared not return to the same landing place, but the wind was blowing against me and I could not paddle very far. As I was looking for a secure landing place, I saw a sail to north-northeast, which appeared more visible with each passing minute. I was in some doubt as to whether I should wait for them. My hatred of the Yahoo race prevailed and I turned my canoe, paddling back to the same creek from which I had escaped earlier. I would rather trust myself among these natives than live with European Yahoos. I drew my canoe as close as I could to the shore and hid myself behind a stone.

The ship came within half a league before sending her longboat out to take in fresh water from the brook. The seamen found my canoe, and then quickly found me as well, flat on my face behind the stone. They gazed in amazement at my strange dress, my coat made of skins, and my wood-soled shoes. Speaking in Portuguese, they bid me rise and asked me who I was.

Speaking that language well enough, I got to my feet and said that I was a poor Yahoo, banished from the Houyhnhnms, and wished that they would let me go. They were impressed to hear me answer in their language, but were at a loss as to what I meant by Yahoo and Houyhnhnms. They said they were sure that their captain would take me to Lisbon. From there, I could return to my own country. They were curious to know my story, but I told them very little and they decided that my misfortunes had injured my ability to reason.

The captain turned out to be a kind and generous man. He brought me to his cabin, urged me to give some account of myself, and asked me what I would like to eat or drink. I was amazed to hear a Yahoo speak in such a civil tone, but I kept silent. The captain ordered a chicken and some water, then ordered that I be put to bed in a clean cabin. I would not undress, but lay on top of the sheets. After I thought the crew would be at dinner, I stole out of my cabin and tried to leap from the ship and swim for my life. One of the seamen caught me, though, and I was chained to my cabin.

Later, the captain came to me and asked why I had attempted such a desperate act. He assured me that he meant to do well by me, and his tone was so moving that I decided to tell him my story. Afterward though, he looked upon the words I had spoken as some kind of dream. I took great offense at this, forgetting the idea of lying, and insisted that I would never *say the thing that was not.*

After examining my story more carefully, the captain began to believe me. He asked for my word that I would not try to escape again, saying

that otherwise I would have to be kept as a prisoner. I gave him this promise, protesting at the same time that I would suffer great hardships rather than live again among Yahoos.

The rest of our voyage passed without any major events. We arrived at Lisbon on the fifth of November, 1715. The captain took me to his house, where I stayed with him for several days. He was so well-mannered and kind that, in time, I actually began to like his company. He continued to try and convince me to return to my home to live with my wife and children.

Finally, seeing I could do no better, I left Lisbon on the twenty-fourth day of November. My wife and family received me with great surprise and joy, but I must confess that the sight of them filled me with disgust. I had forced myself to tolerate the company of Yahoos, yet my imagination was full of the virtues and ideas of those wonderful Houyhnhnms and the life I had enjoyed there.

At the time of my writing, it is five years since my return to England. Slowly, I have learned to endure, and in some cases even enjoy the company of my Yahoo family. The first money I made upon my return was laid out to buy two young stallions, which I keep in a good stable. I feel my spirits revived by their company. My horses understand me fairly well, and I speak with them at least four hours every day. They are strangers to bridle and saddle, and they live in great friendship with me and each other.

What Do *You* Think?
Questions for Discussion

◆⁓

Have you ever been around a toddler who keeps asking the question "Why?" Does your teacher call on you in class with questions from your homework? Do your parents ask you questions about your day at the dinner table? We are always surrounded by questions that need a specific response. But is it possible to have a question with no right answer?

The following questions are about the book you just read. But this is not a quiz! They are designed to help you look at the people, places, and events in the story from different angles. These questions do not have specific answers. Instead, they might make you think of the story in a completely new way.

Think carefully about each question and enjoy discovering more about this classic story.

1. When Gulliver awakes in Lilliput, he discovers that he has been tied down by men "not six inches high." How would you have reacted in Gulliver's position? What is the strangest experience you have ever had?

2. Almost immediately after reaching Lilliput, Gulliver seems to make an enemy of Skyresh Bolgolam. Why do you think this happens? Have you ever unknowingly made an enemy?

3. Why do you think Gulliver has a constant need to travel? Have you ever felt a similar need? Where would you most like to travel to?

4. Gulliver goes from being the biggest man in the land to the smallest. How would this

make you feel? Would you rather be big or small?

5. Gulliver keeps finding lands within our world that he didn't know existed. Do you think it is possible that such lands are really out there? If you were to create a new world, what would it look like?

6. While in the land of the giants, Gulliver has a number of accidents. Which did you think was the worst? Have you ever had an accident that was not too serious and simply made others laugh? What was it?

7. Gulliver seems to gain a new nickname with each country he visits. What does each of his nicknames mean? Have you ever had a nickname? Who gave it to you?

8. Of all the places Gulliver visits, the only one he wishes to stay in is the land of the Houyhnhnms. Why do you think this is? Have you ever visited a place you never wanted to leave?

9. Once on Luggnagg, Gulliver learns about the Struldbrugs, creatures that live forever. How does his opinion of them change over time? Would you want to live forever? Why or why not?

10. How does Gulliver change from the beginning of the book to the end? What do you suppose he learned from all of his travels? Have you ever learned anything from a trip you took?

Afterword

by Arthur Pober, EdD

∽

First impressions are important.

Whether we are meeting new people, going to new places, or picking up a book unknown to us, first impressions count for a lot. They can lead to warm, lasting memories or can make us shy away from any future encounters.

Can you recall your own first impressions and earliest memories of reading the classics?

Do you remember wading through pages and pages of text to prepare for an exam? Or were you the child who hid under the blanket to read with a flashlight, joining forces with Robin Hood to save Maid Marian? Do you remember only how long it took you to read a lengthy novel such as *Little Women*? Or did you become best friends with the March sisters?

Even for a gifted young reader, getting through long chapters with dense language can easily become overwhelming and can obscure the richness of the story and its characters. Reading an abridged, newly crafted version of a classic novel can be the gentle introduction a child needs to explore the characters and story line without the frustration of difficult vocabulary and complex themes.

Reading an abridged version of a classic novel gives the young reader a sense of independence and the satisfaction of finishing a "grown-up" book. And when a child is engaged with and inspired by a classic story, the tone is set for further exploration of the story's themes, characters, history, and details. As a child's reading skills advance, the desire to tackle the original, unabridged version of the story will naturally emerge.

If made accessible to young readers, these stories can become invaluable tools for understanding themselves in the context of their families and social environments. This is why the *Classic Starts* series includes questions that stimulate discussion regarding the impact and social relevance of the characters and stories today. These questions can foster lively conversations between children and their parents or teachers. When we look at the issues, values, and standards of past times in terms of how we live now, we can appreciate literature's classic tales in a very personal and engaging way.

Share your love of reading the classics with a young child, and introduce an imaginary world real enough to last a lifetime.

Dr. Arthur Pober, EdD

Dr. Arthur Pober has spent more than twenty years in the fields of early-childhood and gifted education. He is the former principal of one of the world's oldest laboratory schools for gifted youngsters, Hunter College Elementary School, and former Director of Magnet Schools for the Gifted and Talented for more than 25,000 youngsters in New York City.

Dr. Pober is a recognized authority in the areas of media and child protection and is currently the U.S. representative to the European Institute for the Media and European Advertising Standards Alliance.

Explore these wonderful stories in our
Classic Starts™ library.

20,000 Leagues Under the Sea
The Adventures of Huckleberry Finn
The Adventures of Robin Hood
The Adventures of Sherlock Holmes
The Adventures of Tom Sawyer
Alice in Wonderland & Through the Looking Glass
Anne of Avonlea
Anne of Green Gables
Arabian Nights
Around the World in 80 Days
Black Beauty
The Call of the Wild
Dracula
The Five Litter Peppers and How They Grew
Frankenstein
Gulliver's Travels
Heidi
The Hunchback of Notre-Dame
The Jungle Book
The Last of the Mohicans
Little Lord Fauntleroy

Little Men

A Little Princess

Little Women

The Man in the Iron Mask

Oliver Twis

Peter Pant

The Phantom of the Opera

Pinocchio

Pollyanna

The Prince and the Pauper

Rebecca of Sunnybrook Farm

The Red Badge of Courage

Robinson Crusoe

The Secret Garden

The Story of King Arthur and His Knights

The Strange Case of Dr. Jekyll and Mr. Hyde

The Swiss Family Robinson

The Three Musketeers

The Time Machine

Treasure Island

The Voyages of Doctor Dolittle

The War of the Worlds

White Fang

The Wind in the Willows